PRESENTED TO

_____

BY

_____

DATE

_____

The Driving Force

Handling the Curves in Life

MIKE HEMBREE

Contents

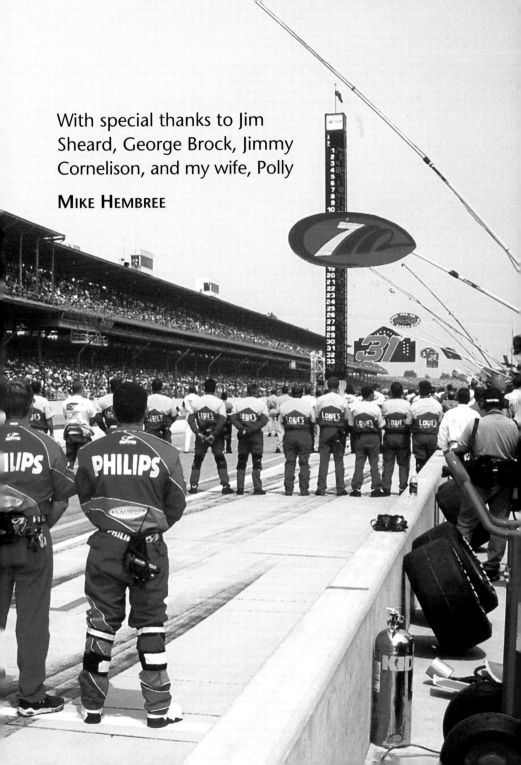

With special thanks to Jim
Sheard, George Brock, Jimmy
Cornelison, and my wife, Polly

MIKE HEMBREE

FOREWORD

I plead guilty to the charge of being a competitive guy. In football or car racing, the urge to compete gets me fired up about life.

Competitive racing involves tight passes and split-second timing, and it requires minute-by-minute courage and an uncompromising willingness to seize the moment. The sport demands a strong character, endurance, and nerves of steel—for drivers and team members!

In many ways, the boldness of racing is like walking with the Lord. Drivers willingly endure g-forces at every turn for hundreds of laps, staying alert for that momentary opening that will help them gain a position. Christians, too, strive to focus on God's leading in their lives, hoping to be prepared when His plan comes into view. Like the Winston Cup® drivers, Christians try to stay on the right line and out of trouble, especially when the metal starts flying and the caution flag comes out.

Both Christians and drivers seek victory at the finish line. But timing is everything, and patience is the best protection. Years of experience have taught me that God reserves the very best for those who leave the timing to Him; our success is in His tender care. From the Super Bowl or Victory Lane to losses at every turn, I've come to understand that winning or losing, God never changes. He shows no shadow of turning. He loves His children as much when they're on the top as when they're on the bottom.

Cast your lot with the God who calls you to boldly walk with Him. He will never leave your side.

Joe Gibbs
January 2000

No sport is more electric than NASCAR® racing.

February through November, Winston Cup drivers engage in some of the most intense, consistently fierce competition in the world of sport.

They race on half-mile ovals where fender-to-fender bumping is normal policy. They chase each other on mammoth, two hundred miles per hour superspeedways where a single wrong move can cause a calamity. In a swirl of vibrant color, they face deafening noise and pervasive danger.

The thunder of the race and the colors of the show, combined with the quality of the competition and personalities of the drivers, have made stock car racing one of the most popular spectator sports in the world. The Winston Cup series attracts more than six million fans to speedways from New Hampshire to California and Michigan to Florida. Millions more who have never attended a race have become devoted fans through television and other media coverage.

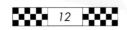

Fueled by the explosive gains in television viewership, the sport has seen unprecedented expansion in facility enhancements and news media exposure; *Sports Illustrated* recently called NASCAR racing "America's hottest sport."

Not surprisingly, the leading drivers in this No. 1 form of auto racing are white-hot celebrities. Fans follow their every move, wait in long lines for an autograph, and buy hats, T-shirts, and model cars emblazoned with their favorite driver's number and image.

Success, however, is not an easy course. Of the thousands of qualified drivers who compete, only a few dozen make it to the top rung of racing. The forty to fifty drivers who travel the roads of the Winston Cup face a long list of hurdles and pressures in a multitude of environments. Short tracks require patience and smart driving, while the huge, sprawling oval tracks call for nearly unlimited speed and split-second reactions.

The drivers also deal with abusive anti-fans, and they must meet demanding schedules that satisfy team owners, company sponsors, and news media members.

Their struggles and successes are not so dissimilar to the curves and surprises of the Christian walk, however. Though most of us will never drive in a Winston Cup race, the qualities needed to steer through life are much the same as those sought in this highly competitive world.

Just as drivers must focus constantly on the way ahead, followers of Christ must concentrate on God's plan for their daily lives. We should walk through our days with a confident stride, bold in the knowledge that He holds our future. We are called to be as courageous as the Winston Cup driver who puts his life on the line every time he steps into a race car.

Contrary to its appearance as a fast-forward sport, racing also rewards patience. Knowing when to pass and where to make a move are as important as being the fastest. In our own fast-moving lives, we must also be patient. God often teaches us to wait on Him as He guides us in making the best decisions.

The qualities of a good race car driver are proven principles of the Christ-centered life. As you read this book and enjoy the colorful accounts from the world of racing, it is my hope that you will also find real-life applications to the daily challenges every Christian faces.

Mike Hembree
January 2000

CHAPTER ONE

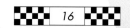

Courage

BE STRONG
AND OF GOOD COURAGE.

(DEUTERONOMY 31:6)

Jeff Gordon drives for one of the most successful teams in motor sports and has a résumé that begins at age five. He started his career by racing quarter-midget cars and steadily progressed through increasingly difficult levels of competition until he arrived on the NASCAR Winston Cup scene late in 1992.

Since then, Gordon has been a soaring rocket, winning races at an unprecedented clip and stacking championships in his column. His impact has been unlike that of any other young driver entering the major leagues of auto racing.

In 1997 and 1999, Gordon illustrated the depth of his talent with two sensational moves that led to victories in the Daytona 500, stock car racing's biggest event. They were among the most courageous victory runs in recent racing history.

In the twilight laps of the 1997 500, Gordon made what will be remembered as one of the boldest passes in the race's forty-year history. Veteran Bill Elliott held the lead and was driving low near the entrance to the first turn—one of the fastest spots on the speedway—when Gordon cut to the inside of Elliott. Then, going very low at the edge of the asphalt in the turn, he thundered past Elliott.

A few minutes later, Gordon achieved his first Daytona 500 victory.

Two years later, as if to show that the first time wasn't a fluke, Gordon made another bold pass in the same spot and in similar circumstances.

Wallace was leading the race in a pack of tight traffic, with Gordon among those in his wake. Gordon decided to try to move to the front while entering the first turn area, but his strategy was complicated by the fact that the much slower car of Ricky Rudd was rolling along out of the racing groove on the low part of the track.

Gordon ran to the inside, squeezed between the cars of Rudd and Wallace, made the pass stick, and burst into first place. With everybody wondering how he had done it, Gordon drove on to the checkered flag, another Daytona 500 victory in hand.

His boldness had produced fruit again.

Courage consists not in blindly overlooking danger but in meeting it with the eyes open.

JEAN PAUL

Accepting the Challenge

*Be strong and of good courage; do not be afraid,
nor be dismayed, for the Lord your God is with you
wherever you go.*
JOSHUA 1:9

Bold moves are as important for racers as they are for followers of Christ. Christians are called to be courageous.

One of the most beloved Bible stories is that of David and Goliath—a boy of Bethlehem and a giant of the Philistines (1 Sam. 16–17). Even Israel's fiercest warriors feared Goliath, but David, strengthened by God's presence in his life, accepted the challenge.

A single stone from David's sling dropped Goliath; the giant's death led the Israeli army to victory.

David showed a simple boldness, stepping forward when no one else would. It was the sort of courage inspired by a prayerful, intense relationship with God.

We, too, have been empowered with the Holy Spirit to boldly walk with Him.

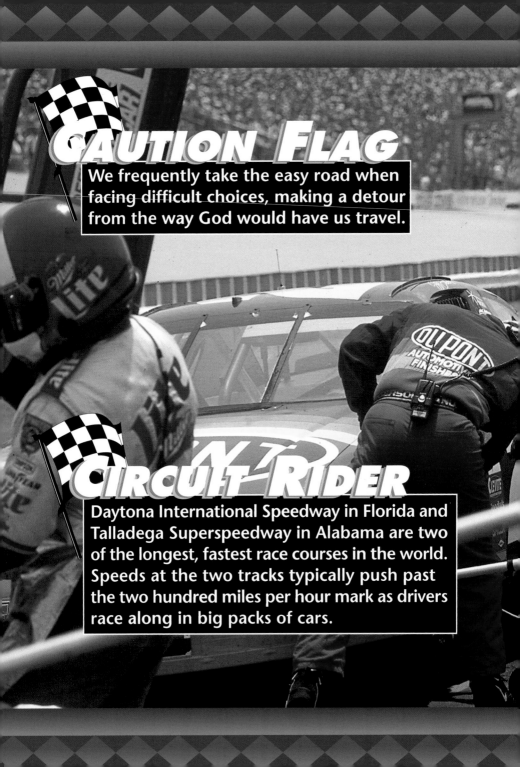

CAUTION FLAG

We frequently take the easy road when facing difficult choices, making a detour from the way God would have us travel.

CIRCUIT RIDER

Daytona International Speedway in Florida and Talladega Superspeedway in Alabama are two of the longest, fastest race courses in the world. Speeds at the two tracks typically push past the two hundred miles per hour mark as drivers race along in big packs of cars.

PIT STOP

When we go in the strength of the Lord, we carry the power of boldness, a sure answer to every adversary.

CHAPTER TWO

Perseverance

LET US RUN WITH PERSEVERANCE THE RACE MARKED OUT FOR US. *(HEBREWS 12:1, NIV)*

For much of the last quarter-century of auto racing, few sights in the sport have been as chilling as Dale Earnhardt's black No. 3 Chevrolet filling a competitor's rear-view mirror.

Earnhardt's racing style is the essence of aggressive. In the peak years of his career, the multi-Winston Cup champion found no peer to his smart, bullish, run-to-the-front driving. More than a few competitors felt the thump of Earnhardt's front bumper as he propelled through rows of traffic to first place.

Earnhardt's thrilling experiences in racing include a string of championships, dozens of victories with last-lap power moves, and, finally, the 1998 win in the Daytona 500.

But few episodes illustrate the depth of Earnhardt's character like one he experienced in the summer of 1996.

The Winston Cup tour had visited Talladega Superspeedway in Alabama for a midsummer race, and the day turned dangerous. Earnhardt, usually masterful at avoiding accidents, was swept into one of the huge track's dangerous multicar wrecks. His car rolled over and was heavily damaged. Earnhardt, too, was wounded: he had a broken collarbone and a cracked sternum—very painful injuries, especially for a man planning to drive a race car again very soon.

But two weeks later, Earnhardt took his place in the driver's seat of the Chevrolet on the Watkins Glen road course in New York. Still in the early stages of healing, Earnhardt sat uncomfortably in the car as he prepared to run a qualifying lap. The twisting road course would be particularly difficult for a racer with shoulder and chest injuries.

Earnhardt, reaching deep for the grit that had fueled so much of his career, did the near impossible. He was the fastest driver on the track that day, winning the pole position for the race and setting a track-record speed in the process.

His career has been filled with highlights, but that day, Earnhardt displayed the perseverance that drove him to the top.

Completing the Race

I can do all things through Christ who strengthens m
PHILIPPIANS 4:13

In Romans 5:3, Paul the Apostle offers hope to Christians who persevere under trials. He says that we can "glory in tribulations, knowing that tribulation produces perseverance, and perseverance, character; and character, hope."

God called Paul to a life of suffering, yet he persevered because his trials made him stronger and drew him closer to the Lord. After his first sermon, Paul had to escape in a basket over a wall. During his three successful missionary journeys, he was stripped and beaten, stoned and left for dead, shipwrecked, and imprisoned many times.

But even while imprisoned, Paul wrote encouraging letters to early Christian churches. He did not quit when he faced difficulties. He persevered, endured troubles, and served God until the end. Even when facing execution, he was able to say, "I have fought the good fight, I have finished the race, I have kept the faith" (2 Tim. 4:7).

One of the essential characteristics of a faithful servant of Christ is perseverance in the midst of difficulties.

CAUTION FLAG

Christianity will not take us down an easy road. The way involves hardships and suffering, but we persevere because Christ has promised to walk with us through the pain.

CIRCUIT RIDER

Some of the toughest racing of the long Winston Cup season occurs in the summer months when on-track temperatures soar and heat reaches dangerous levels inside the tight cockpits of the race cars.

PIT STOP

When we do not try to squirm out of our problems, our faith has a chance to grow.

CHAPTER THREE

Determination

INDEED WE COUNT THEM BLESSED WHO ENDURE.

(JAMES 5:11)

The calendar said it was fall, but no one at Martinsville Speedway in southern Virginia on September 27, 1998, was dressed for autumn chill.

As the green flag fell to mark the start of the NAPA 500, temperatures boiled into the mid '90s. The breeze was almost nonexistent.

The conditions were, at best, difficult and, at worst, dangerous for the forty-three drivers racing five hundred laps on the flat, half-mile track. The heat generated by powerful racing engines, the tight cockpits of the cars, and the sun-beaten asphalt of the speedway surface seemed to melt together, making the drivers feel like roasts in an oven.

Virtually all drivers use some sort of cooling system in their cars on hot and humid afternoons; typically, the systems circulate cool, refreshing air through the drivers' helmets. However, Ricky Rudd, a veteran driver from Chesapeake, Virginia, discovered that his cooling system had malfunctioned—and he was only on lap five, with 495 long laps and more than three hours of red-hot racing remaining.

Rudd immediately radioed his crew members, telling them to ask the first driver who fell out of the race to stand by as a replacement—a standard practice for drivers who leave a race because of illness or injury.

In this type of situation, Rudd probably would have driven only a portion of the race, enduring the heat until he needed a fresh replacement. But this day would not be typical.

Rudd determined in the race's very early laps that he had a particularly strong car, one he figured was good enough to win the race. And he knew that chance probably would disappear if he stopped long enough in the pits for a driver change.

So, despite conditions that were brutally hot, Rudd held fast. Determined to come in first, he stayed in the car all the way—and won the race by .53 of a second. In victory lane, he had to be helped from the car and given oxygen. He was treated for burns on his lower back and needed thirty minutes to recover before participating in the victory celebration.

On a day in which it would have been easy to give up, Ricky Rudd chose the more difficult—and more rewarding—path. Despite obstacles, he was determined to score his first victory of the season.

Go After the Prize

Let us run with endurance the race that is set before us.
HEBREWS 12:1

In First Corinthians, Paul advises us to be committed to the "race" so that we will win the heavenly prize: "a crown that will last forever" (9:24–25). In describing his own dedication to the Christian walk, Paul says, "Therefore I do not run like a man running aimlessly; I do not fight like a man beating the air. No, I beat my body and make it my slave so that after I have preached to others, I myself will not be disqualified for the prize" (9:26–27).

Paul makes it clear that success does not come without determination and persistence. The easy approach is usually not the best. Instead, we should devote all that we have to God and the study of His Word.

We need to put on God's full armor. The way occasionally may be rough, but the reward is great.

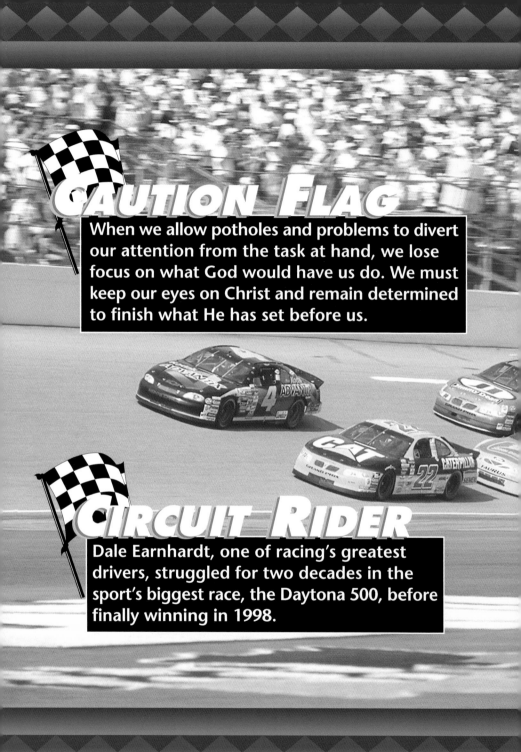

CAUTION FLAG

When we allow potholes and problems to divert our attention from the task at hand, we lose focus on what God would have us do. We must keep our eyes on Christ and remain determined to finish what He has set before us.

CIRCUIT RIDER

Dale Earnhardt, one of racing's greatest drivers, struggled for two decades in the sport's biggest race, the Daytona 500, before finally winning in 1998.

PIT STOP

We can reach God's victory by remaining faithful to Him and staying the course, even under pressure.

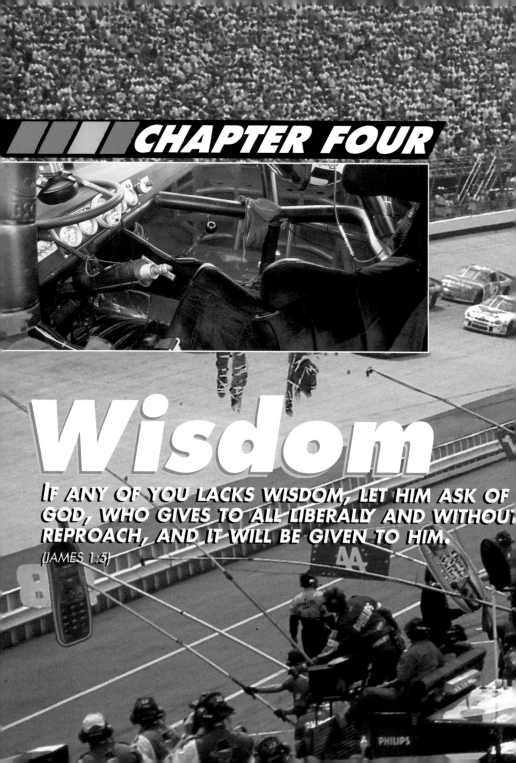

CHAPTER FOUR

Wisdom

IF ANY OF YOU LACKS WISDOM, LET HIM ASK OF GOD, WHO GIVES TO ALL LIBERALLY AND WITHOUT REPROACH, AND IT WILL BE GIVEN TO HIM.

(JAMES 1:5)

Retired driver David Pearson is remembered as one of the most intelligent racers in NASCAR history.

A winner 105 times, Pearson was a rousing success in Winston Cup racing primarily because of his uncanny ability to outsmart the competition. After dozens of victories, he became known as the Silver Fox, a nickname inspired, in part, by his graying hair but mostly by the way he used strategy and intelligence to win races.

Although Pearson could run at the front—and frequently did—he built a reputation for staying back in the pack, saving the strength of his equipment until the final quarter of a race, and then hunting the lead. In the twilight of the day, with everything on the line, he would suddenly appear in the rearview mirror of the leader, ready to make his planned move into first place. Undoubtedly, Pearson scored the biggest wins of his career with his head instead of his right foot.

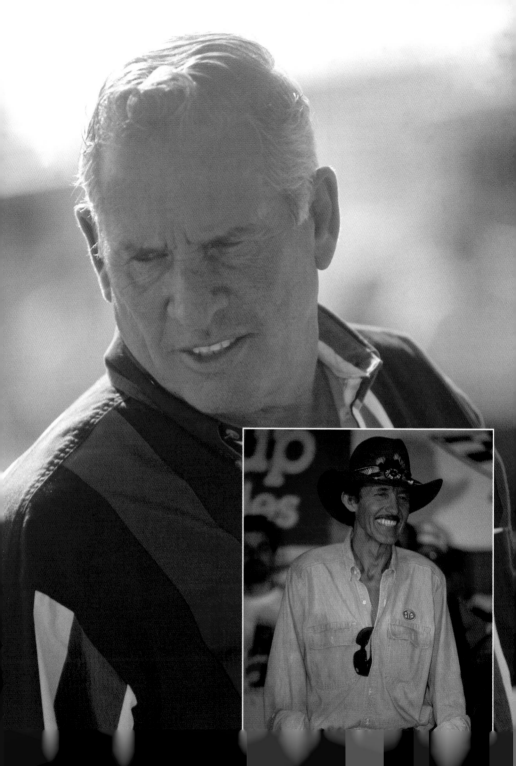

In the mid 1970s, both Pearson and Richard Petty were near the peaks of their careers. On dozens of occasions, races developed into Petty-Pearson duels for victory. This was the case when the Winston Cup drivers arrived at Daytona International Speedway for the Daytona 500 in February 1976. Though Petty and Pearson were already the acknowledged giants of the sport, by day's end, their legends would grow even more significantly.

Petty held the lead in the season's biggest race with thirteen laps to go. He kept his familiar red and blue car out in front until the last lap, when Pearson passed him for the lead on the backstretch. But Pearson drifted high entering turn three, leaving Petty an opening to retake the lead.

As they exited turn four with the checkered flag in sight, their cars bumped, sending them both skidding into the outside wall and then onto the grass beside the track. Both cars came to a stop just short of the finish line.

Pearson, despite the violence of the wreck and the pressure of the moment, didn't stop thinking. As his battered car slid across the grass, he depressed the clutch to prevent the engine from stalling. As Petty struggled to return to the track, Pearson put his car in gear, drove onto the racing surface, and puttered across the finish line at about twenty miles per hour to win the race.

Quick thinking and the wisdom gained from years of racing gave Pearson the biggest checkered flag of his career.

I've been racing all my life. Through the experience of doing the right thing and the wrong thing, I've learned what would be the best thing to do throughout the race.

MARK MARTIN

God's Wisdom

The fear of the Lord is the beginning of wisdom; a good understanding have all those who do His commandme

Knowing the right thing to do at the proper time is invaluable to every Christian.

This particular gift was granted to young King Solomon. When God instructed Solomon to ask for anything he wanted, Solomon chose wisdom instead of long life or possessions. But God rewarded Solomon's humble request not only with wisdom but also with riches and honor. He was promised a long life, as well, if he walked in the ways of God (I Kings 3:1–14).

Solomon soon became the wisest man who ever lived. Kings and dignitaries came to Israel bringing their treasures just to witness the wisdom of Solomon.

However, later in life, Solomon made mistakes. Against the Lord's commands, he married many foreign wives who influenced him to turn his heart toward idolatry, and he lost his fellowship with God. Although God gave Solomon great wisdom, he failed to use it well (11:1–10).

We can make the right decisions in our own lives when we ask God to give us the wisdom to know what to do and the courage to follow through on it. God blesses those who are willing to walk in His ways.

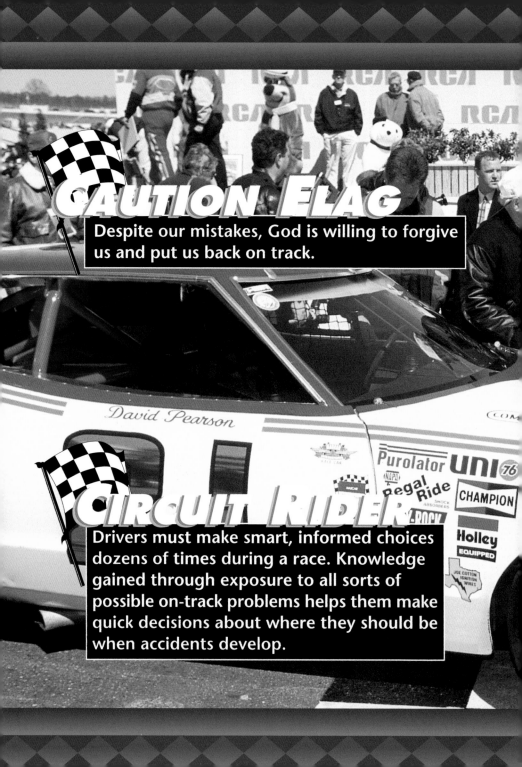

CAUTION FLAG

Despite our mistakes, God is willing to forgive us and put us back on track.

CIRCUIT RIDER

Drivers must make smart, informed choices dozens of times during a race. Knowledge gained through exposure to all sorts of possible on-track problems helps them make quick decisions about where they should be when accidents develop.

PIT STOP

Seeking God's wisdom each day helps us avoid the detours of tomorrow.

CHAPTER FIVE

Experience

IN EVERYTHING SET THEM AN EXAMPLE
BY DOING WHAT IS GOOD.

(TITUS 2:7, NIV)

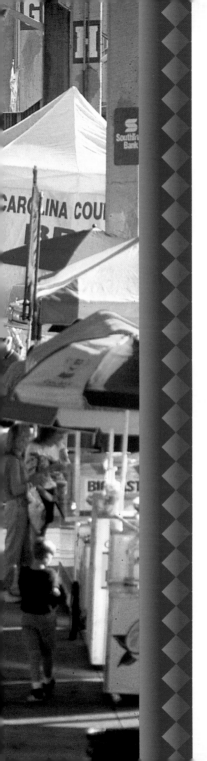

Over the years, one of the uncontested truths of Winston Cup racing has been that experience goes before a victory.

Unlike most other sports, auto racing rewards longevity. While many pro basketball players are limping along at age thirty-eight, stock car racers, in many cases, are about to step into their prime at that age. Typically, a race car driver's most productive years are between the ages of thirty-five and forty-five, and drivers routinely race well into their fifties.

At the "ripe old age" of forty-seven, Dick Trickle won the Winston Cup rookie of the year award. And Harry Gant, one of stock car racing's most popular drivers, stretched the idea of success at an "advanced" age to the extreme. He did something remarkable—won four straight races—at the age of fifty-one in 1991.

Gant, who retired in 1994, scored his quartet of consecutive victories at four of NASCAR's more formidable tracks.

The streak began at Darlington Raceway in South Carolina. NASCAR's oldest superspeedway, Darlington is oddly shaped and is considered ornery. Its tight turns and narrow passing lanes are like magnets for wrecks. But Gant, calling on years of experience at the old track, won the Southern 500 by eleven seconds.

Less than a week later, Gant took the lead late in the race and outran Davey Allison to win at the Richmond International Raceway in Virginia. Then, at Dover Downs International Speedway, a highly banked super-fast, one-mile track in Delaware, Gant faced a strenuous test of endurance and skill. Dover is not for the meek and mild, but Gant was ready. Of the final 330 laps of a grueling 500, he led in 326. At day's end, he had lapped the rest of the field, easily winning his third straight victory.

Gant then would tie the NASCAR record for most consecutive wins at the tour's next stop—Martinsville Speedway in Virginia. At .526 of a mile, it is the shortest Winston Cup track and often one of the most frustrating.

A typical race day at Martinsville is filled with fender-banging and bumper-beating as drivers maneuver around the tight oval. Drivers often call on prior understanding to counter what could be a frustrating afternoon.

Gant led early in the race until he suffered an accident. After dropping into the pits several times for repairs, he bounced back and returned to the action at the front. He took the lead with forty-five laps to go and reached the checkered flag first, stretching his winning streak to four.

Gant showed, over a series of tough races, that experience means as much as any other factor in racing to the front.

I think I'm more of a thinking-type driver now. I used to be more of a fly-by-the-seat-of-your-pants driver. But I've learned to tailor that with the importance of finishing races.

CHAD LITTLE

Mature in Christ

Does not long life bring understanding?

JOB 12:12 (NIV)

Some people come to know Christ at the young age of six, while others welcome a relationship with Him at the ages of twenty, fifty, eighty, or older. Regardless of our time of life, His spirit lives in everyone who believes in Him.

Though spiritual maturity is not always determined by age, many older Christians can be wonderful examples for younger Christians. They have experienced hardships that have drawn them closer to God, and they have seen the hand of God in their lives and the lives of others.

Christians who have known Christ for many decades are often wonderful people of prayer. They have gathered God's wisdom and understanding. Seek them out.

CAUTION FLAG

We sometimes make the mistake of thinking that what is presented to us is the best choice without examining all of the possibilities.

CIRCUIT RIDER

NASCAR's trickiest tracks—Darlington Raceway, Bristol Motor Speedway, and Pocono International Raceway—often are conquered by drivers who have many years of experience on the circuit.

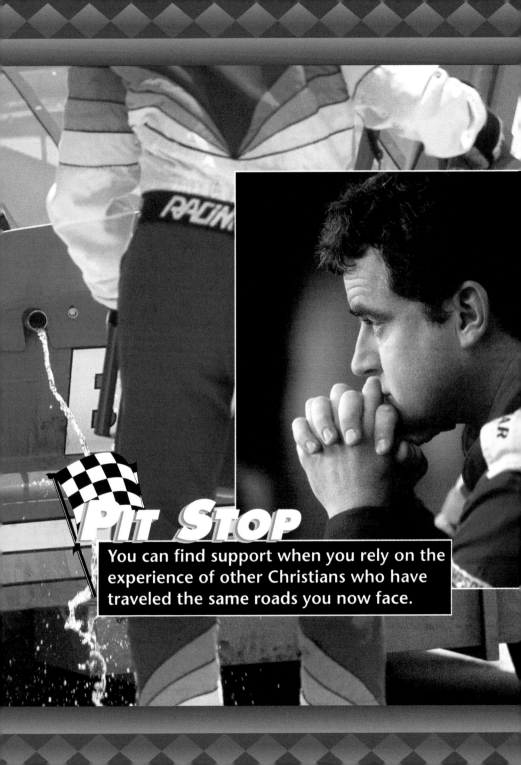

PIT STOP

You can find support when you rely on the experience of other Christians who have traveled the same roads you now face.

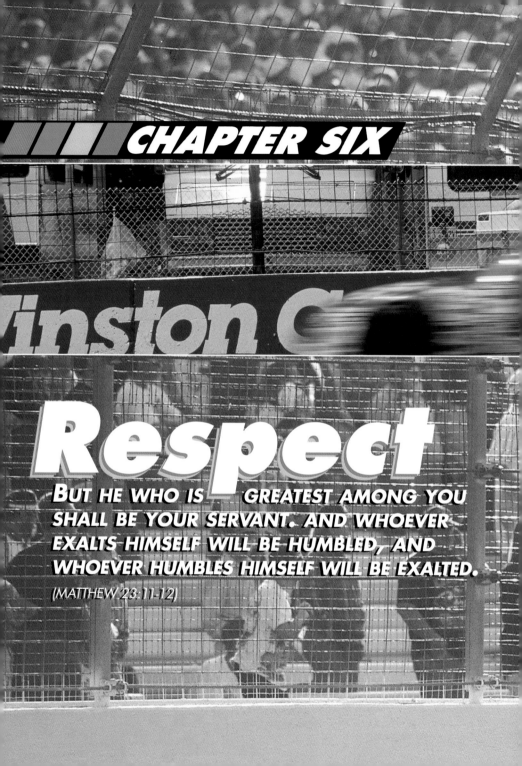

CHAPTER SIX

Winston C

Respect

BUT HE WHO IS GREATEST AMONG YOU SHALL BE YOUR SERVANT. AND WHOEVER EXALTS HIMSELF WILL BE HUMBLED, AND WHOEVER HUMBLES HIMSELF WILL BE EXALTED.

(MATTHEW 23:11-12)

The final week of the 1997 Winston Cup championship was one of the most intense in stock car racing history.

It was the season's last race, the NAPA 500 at Atlanta Motor Speedway, and three of the sport's best drivers—Jeff Gordon, Dale Jarrett, and Mark Martin—were vying to win the national championship. Though Gordon won the title in 1995, Jarrett and Martin were shooting for their first championships.

With money and prestige on the line and sponsors waiting to align themselves with the new champion, the brutal pressure affected everyone. Mechanics worked overtime to make sure their driver's car was as close to perfect as possible. Engine builders checked and double-checked every part, and racing teams wrote and rewrote their strategy in long planning sessions.

The unusually close race for the championship had all the drama of the seventh game of the World Series or the morning of the Masters' final round. It brought swarms of news media representatives to the race site in suburban

Atlanta. Every seat in the speedway's sprawling grandstands was sold.

In the middle of all of the commotion—with team members, media representatives, and fans pulling them in all directions—Gordon, Jarrett, and Martin did a remarkable thing. Instead of glaring at each other across a field of combat, instead of posturing and talking tough about what might happen in the race, they met with Motor Racing Outreach chaplain Max Helton and prayed together.

Gordon remembers the moment as one of the highlights of his racing career.

"It was really neat because it was three guys who had faith in God," he said. "We all wanted to win, but I think we were all genuinely happy for whoever did win. That makes it tough to go out and race against those guys, but it helps to know that you're content with whatever the results are."

The prayer session, suggested by Jarrett, came at the conclusion of a Bible study the night before the race. Helton said, "They held hands, and each one prayed out loud that everyone would have a good race tomorrow. It was an amazing experience, and one of the greatest things I've ever been involved in. And I was just sort of a bystander."

Gordon finished seventeenth in the race, good enough to win the championship by fourteen points over Jarrett and twenty-nine over Martin.

One man practicing sportsmanship is far better than fifty preaching it.
KNUTE ROCKNE

A Respect for Others

Be devoted to one another in brotherly love.

Honor one another above yourselves.

ROMANS 12:10 (NIV)

Athletes who sometimes squabble over money and fame are not unlike Christians who occasionally behave in the same manner. James and John, the sons of Zebedee, angered the other disciples when they asked Jesus for a special place of honor beside Him in His coming kingdom (Mark 10:35–37). Jesus then explained that for someone to become great, he must become a servant of others.

God's view of success involves humility and service, the exact opposite of the world's view. As we approach life, we can choose to concentrate on what's best for ourselves or we can choose to follow Jesus and put others first.

We should seek to show a genuine interest in others and look for opportunities to demonstrate a true respect for others.

CAUTION FLAG

Our aim is to please God, not ourselves. Selfish ambition prevents God from using us to bless others.

CIRCUIT RIDER

Ned Jarrett shared his testimony with a Methodist youth group before driving in the 1965 Southern 500 in Darlington, South Carolina. He later won the race by fourteen laps (19.25 miles), a record victory-margin.

PIT STOP

In the Christian perspective, the last become first, and servants become kings.

CHAPTER SEVEN

Patience

BEAR FRUIT WITH PATIENCE. (LUKE 8:15)

By definition, auto racing is all about going as fast as possible, getting every last bit of horsepower from the engine, and pushing a race car to its limits—and sometimes beyond.

It might seem surprising, then, that one of the primary attributes of the successful race car driver is patience.

The racer who storms through the field with little regard for planning his next move often finds himself bounced into the wall or squeezed in tight traffic. Driving a race car as fast as it will go often is not the best way to win a race.

"The harder you drive, the more you hurt your brakes and kill your tires," said Kenny Wallace, referring to the half-mile Martinsville Speedway. "You've got to sit back in your seat and drive, realizing that you've got five hundred laps to make."

On a small, flat track like Martinsville, brakes become the prevailing factor instead of speed. A driver who roars along too fast early in the race can burn up his brakes by having to slow repeatedly in the track's tight turns. Patience—knowing the right time to try to pass without abusing the car—is crucial.

Patience also is a particularly valuable commodity at Daytona and Talladega, the circuit's two biggest tracks. On these huge ovals, cars race within inches of each other at speeds of two hundred miles per hour and more. A wrong move can be disastrous.

"I can't begin to describe how much patience you have to have," said Bobby Hamilton, who constantly reflects on his next move before he makes it. "I always know who the three or four guys around me are, and I'm always looking a turn ahead."

Patience also is critical over the long run of the season. On a circuit that stretches from coast to coast and February to November, pitfalls and problems are bound to occur.

"You have to have patience and understanding that not every race is going to go the way you want it to," said Jeff Burton. "Not every lap is going [to go] the way you want it to. Don't let those negatives mess you up and make you do things out of anger or emotion."

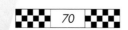

To know how to wait is the great secret of success.
JOSEPH D. MAISTRE

God's Perfect Timing

★ DAYTONA ★

*But those who wait on the Lord shall renew their stren,
shall mount up with wings like eagles, they shall run a
weary, they shall walk and not faint.*
ISAIAH 40:31

If we are to realize the unique blessings God has for us, we must patiently trust His timing and submit to His will.

Mary, the mother of Jesus, trusted God's perfect timing in the face of great risk. God sent His messenger Gabriel to tell Mary she would give birth to the Savior of the world by the miraculous power of the Holy Spirit. Mary, who was eagerly awaiting her marriage to Joseph, could have complained that her husband-to-be might reject her or that her family might disown her. She could have asked, "Who will believe that I am a virgin?" Instead, she simply answered, "I am the Lord's servant. May it be to me as you have said" (Luke 1:38, NIV).

May God give us the patient, submissive spirit of Mary when His timing conflicts with our own.

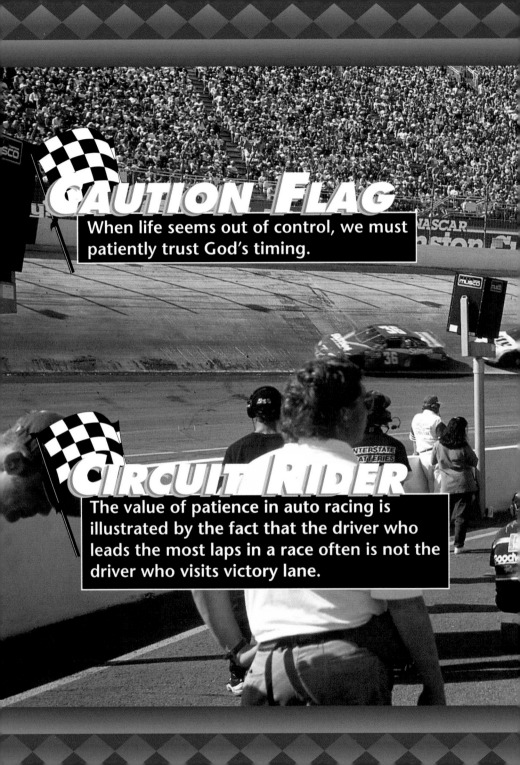

CAUTION FLAG

When life seems out of control, we must patiently trust God's timing.

CIRCUIT RIDER

The value of patience in auto racing is illustrated by the fact that the driver who leads the most laps in a race often is not the driver who visits victory lane.

PIT STOP

Disruptions in our lives can actually be blessings in disguise if we patiently submit to God's will.

CHAPTER EIGHT

Vision

**YOUR WORD IS A LAMP TO MY FEET
AND A LIGHT TO MY PATH.**
(PSALM 119:105)

Winston Cup drivers race at astonishing speeds and in tight competition, placing them only inches from other drivers and the concrete walls surrounding the track.

During a race, events happen quickly. Engines explode. Cars spin. Wrecks erupt. The successful driver, then, must worry not only about his immediate surroundings but also about what is happening in front of him, in the next group of cars.

In essence, he must have good vision.

"Every track allows you to see something different," said Jeff Burton. "What you try to do is look at what's in front of you, but you look beyond that. I try to focus on the car that's in front of me and what I have to do to beat him, but I also take a look ahead.

"I can be looking at the car directly in front of me, and something can happen in the turn ahead and it will catch my eye. Being able to catch things like that out of the corner of your eye is real important."

Race circumstances also often dictate the visual landscape for drivers.

"If I'm in a pack of cars, I pay a lot more attention to what's going on right around me," explained Dale Jarrett. "But if I'm only racing one or two guys, then I'm looking much further ahead."

Even while driving at speeds approaching two hundred miles per hour, drivers are plotting strategy and mapping out logistics as they turn laps. By watching the traffic in front of them, they can pick out the best places to attempt a pass, and as they enter one turn, they can take a quick glance into the next turn to analyze the task ahead.

Vision also impacts the driver's lap speed, a critical element in gaining ground on the competition. If a driver finds a line on the track that is particularly fast, he wants to continue running that line as closely as possible.

"You have to focus on the line you want to run," said Tony Stewart. "If you miss your line a little, it can be bad for you. You really have to concentrate and really look at the line that you want to enter the corner with. Once you get there, you're looking at how you want to exit."

At some tracks, this process is repeated five hundred times, lap after lap after lap.

You have to focus as far ahead of you as you can.
DERRIKE COPE

A *Spiritual* Outlook

Blessed are those who have not seen and yet have believed.
JOHN 20:29

What keen eyesight is to the driver, spiritual vision is to followers of Christ.

Spiritual vision comes from reading God's Word. The Psalmist says God's Word is a lamp unto our feet and a light unto our path. In the Bible, we find instruction for daily living. Life is fragile, uncertain, and perplexing, but God gives comfort and assurance of His care even though we may not know the reason for every problem or difficult circumstance.

Our spiritual vision can be impaired when we attempt to face the troubles of life without applying His Word. But the Bible gives us wisdom, for only God can see beyond the curve and around the bend of our lives. He will keep us in tune and help us through to the finish line.

CAUTION FLAG

Our vision can be impaired by prejudice, fear, or selfish ambition. God's Word will help us clearly see these dangers in our lives.

CIRCUIT RIDER

Alan Kulwicki shocked many in racing when he turned down an offer to drive for legendary car owner Junior Johnson in 1991. But Kulwicki had a dream for the future. And he saw it fulfilled. He drove his own cars to the Winston Cup championship in 1992.

PIT STOP

God's Word gives us a vision of what God has planned for those who trust Him with their lives.

Heritage

BEHOLD, CHILDREN ARE A HERITAGE FROM THE LORD, THE FRUIT OF THE WOMB IS A REWARD.
(PSALM 127: 3)

NASCAR racing is a family sport in the truest sense.

Garage areas at Winston Cup races often seem like staging areas for big family reunions. Drivers bump into relatives— sometimes while walking to a driver's meeting, sometimes while racing on the track.

Stock car racing is filled with brothers competing against brothers and sons racing in cars owned by their fathers, who also are racers. The sport has a great heritage of family ties.

The Pettys make up racing's First Family. Lee Petty, the patriarch, was a NASCAR pioneer, racing in the Winston Cup series' first event in 1949 and winning champion-ships in the 1950s. His son, Richard, followed him into the sport and became its biggest winner ever. Kyle, Richard's son, worked for the family's team and then became one of the series' most popular drivers. Now Adam, Kyle's son, is working on a Winston Cup career, becoming the first fourth-generation driver in major league stock-car racing.

Then there are the Earnhardts. Ralph Earnhardt raced in NASCAR's early years and won the Late Model Sportsman series championship. His son, Dale, worked on cars in the backyard garage and went on to become one of Winston Cup racing's biggest stars. Now Dale Jr. has started his Winston Cup career, racing the same car number—No. 8—as his grandfather.

The list goes on. The Jarretts, Burtons, Allisons, Waltrips, Pearsons, Labontes, Wallaces, Bodines, Greens, Sadlers.

"You look at all four of us," said Kyle Petty of the four racing Pettys, "and we're four totally different people. The only thing that connects us all is that we love racing."

Occasionally, with so many brothers in the sport, siblings wind up racing each other for wins. It happened in 1999 in Las Vegas when Jeff, the younger of the Burton brothers, caught and passed Ward late in the race to win.

"It's tough racing your brother because you want him to do well, too," Jeff said. "It's different than racing against anybody else, but you still want to win."

You don't raise heroes; you raise sons. And if you treat them like sons, they'll turn out to be heroes, even if it's just in your own eyes.
WALTER SCHIRRA

Hidden Treasures

Children's children are a crown to the aged, and parents are the pride of their children.
PROVERBS 17:6 (NIV)

When a family poses for a portrait together, a sense of pride is often captured on film. Children bear a resemblance to their dad or smile like their mom or one of their grandparents. Hidden from the photo's view are other gifts passed down like valued family relics. Some gifts, like kindness, faith, self-respect, and ambition, are given unaware. Others are given through training, practice, and close association.

Family interests, work, and tradition play a major role in creating a heritage. Psalm 127:3 says children themselves are a heritage, a gift or reward from the Lord. In Proverbs, the writer views grandchildren as the crown of their grandparents and parents as the pride of their children (17:6).

Within our families, God has given us treasures to value, respect, and share.

CAUTION FLAG

Though our bad habits are sometimes passed down to those we love, God will lovingly shape them into Christ-like characteristics if we ask.

CIRCUIT RIDER

In May 1999, Dale Earnhardt Jr. made his Winston Cup debut in the Coca-Cola 600 at Lowe's Motor Speedway near Charlotte, North Carolina. As the son of one of auto racing's most popular and successful drivers, he was under extreme pressure, but he qualified eighth for the race and finished sixteenth.

PIT STOP

The greatest gift we can give to our children is God's love.

CHAPTER TEN

Preparation

PREPARE THE WAY OF THE LORD

(ISAIAH 40:3)

One of the odd truths of auto racing is that much of the potential for success on a particular race day is beyond the reach of the driver.

Once a race begins, it often is too late to correct mistakes in car preparation or mechanical construction. If a car's chassis is out of line or its engine is not performing at peak levels, the driver has little chance of racing for the lead.

A key to victory, then, is the quality of preparation that occurs not only at the race track but also during the weeks and months before the race—in the team's shop. Leading Winston Cup teams typically possess a fleet of cars for use during the season, and each one is prepared to race in one of the different environments of the series.

The Winston Cup schedule includes short half-mile tracks and long, superfast superspeedways of more than two miles in length. The circuit also visits road courses, where the dynamics of car preparation differ significantly from the oval tracks that dominate the schedule.

Winston Cup competition has become so intense that teams need to spend practice time fine-tuning the car, not correcting big problems. If they arrive at a race site and find that their car is not set up correctly for the race, they know to expect major difficulties.

Much of the work, then, occurs in race shops and in test sessions at tracks.

"There are no tricks to this business," driver Michael Waltrip said. "It's hard work, preparation, and communication."

Preparation for the new season, which opens in February at Daytona International Speedway, actually begins months earlier, as the old season is approaching its end. Even during the off-season, dozens of mechanics are hard at work building the chassis, frames, roll cages, engines, and other equipment that will determine the team's level of success in the new year. Improvement is on everyone's mind.

"Every year we make a new mission statement and figure out what we have to do to get better," said Jeff Gordon.

In January, teams travel to Daytona twice to test cars for the Daytona 500. In lap after lap around the 2.5-mile track, one of racing's fastest, drivers put new cars through their paces, trying to wring every last ounce of power from them.

When the Daytona 500 rolls around, they will find out how well prepared they are.

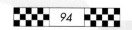

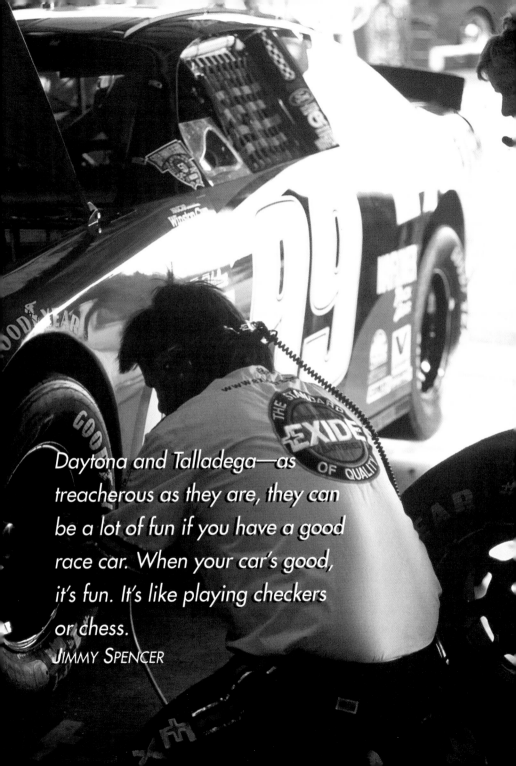

Daytona and Talladega—as treacherous as they are, they can be a lot of fun if you have a good race car. When your car's good, it's fun. It's like playing checkers or chess.
JIMMY SPENCER

Building a Temple

No eye has seen, no ear has heard, no mind has con
what God has prepared for those who love him.
I CORINTHIANS 2:9 (NIV)

God told King David that a temple should be built for worship. He instructed David to prepare the way for his son, Solomon, who would later lead the construction. Because Solomon was young and inexperienced, David made provisions for his son in the planning and construction of the temple.

Solomon received all of the knowledge that God had placed in David's mind for the building of the temple. David gave Solomon the plans for the portico, inner rooms, place of atonement, and other structures. David also provided building materials, workmen, and furnishings for the temple and planned how the worship services would be held. Solomon couldn't have had any better preparation, and he completed the temple in seven years (1 Chron. 28: 11–21; 1 Kings 6:38).

Christians are called to be like David, to prepare the path for others to follow. Through prayer, Bible reading, church affiliation, work, and the way we live our lives, we show others the way to become members of God's family.

CAUTION FLAG

Not every Christian is chosen for a leadership role in God's work, but everyone can prepare to play an important role in His great plan.

CIRCUIT RIDER

Winston Cup racing has become so competitive that teams take special care when preparing for qualifying. A time-trial lap that is only a blink-of-an-eye slower than the competition can result in failure to qualify.

PIT STOP

Countless Christians help to prepare the way for others by building churches, aiding people in distress, and sharing the good news the gospel holds.

CHAPTER ELEVEN

Faith

"BEHOLD, I AM THE LORD, THE GOD OF ALL FLESH. IS THERE ANYTHING TOO HARD FOR ME?"

(JEREMIAH 32:27)

It would have been difficult to pick a worse day for an accident for Bobby Labonte.

Four races into the 1999 season, Labonte had scored three top-five finishes and was riding in second place in the seasonal point standings. A steady driver for several seasons, he appeared to be poised to make a serious run at the national championship, an effort that demands consistency and week-to-week excellence.

Then, on the morning of March 19, while practicing for a race two days away at Darlington Raceway in South Carolina, Labonte suffered one of the hardest accidents of his racing career. He slammed his car into the Darlington wall and fractured his right shoulder blade.

As he stumbled out of his car in severe pain, the promise of the season appeared to be blowing away in the wind.

"I wasn't knocked out, but I was about to pass out when they [the safety workers] got to me," Labonte said. "I was hurting real bad. My blood pressure had dropped very low.

They gave me something because they were afraid I had a punctured lung or a ruptured spleen or kidney."

Labonte was treated at a nearby hospital and returned to the track for a visit later in the day. Although drivers often race with injuries, Labonte wasn't feeling very chipper about what awaited in his immediate future. With one sudden accident, the composure of the season had changed dramatically.

"I honestly thought I wouldn't be able to drive at Darlington, and I thought I'd probably just be able to start the race [then leave the car to a relief driver] at Texas the next week," he said. "It was a pretty rough hit."

Early in the season, with eight months of racing to go, Labonte had to have faith that he and his team could make it through a difficult period and remain in the hunt for the championship.

Ignoring the pain of the injury, Labonte started the race at Darlington, drove forty-five laps in pain, then left the car in the hands of relief driver Matt Kenseth. Kenseth performed admirably, coming home tenth—

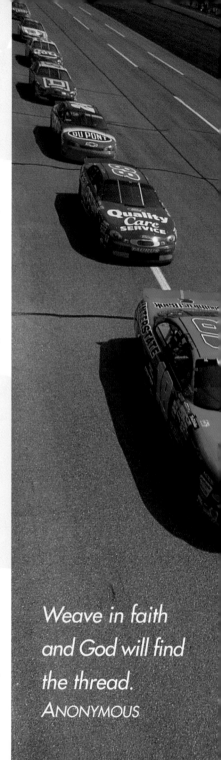

Weave in faith and God will find the thread.
ANONYMOUS

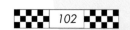

a finish that, under NASCAR rules, was credited to Labonte since he started the car.

By the next week, Labonte was improved enough to tough out the full five hundred miles at Texas Motor Speedway, a physically difficult race track. His first full event since the Darlington wreck, this race presented a major challenge. But Labonte had to believe that he could still get the job done, that he wouldn't hold back when he raced full speed toward an unforgiving wall. Remarkably, he finished third.

Three weeks later, he felt almost mended.

"My stomach was in knots before that [Texas race]," he said. "But once I got comfortable, it was back to normal. I told the crew the best thing I could have done was get back out in the car."

The season rolled on for Labonte, the crisis averted.

Faith: A Guiding Force

*Now faith is the substance of things hoped for,
the evidence of things not seen.*

HEBREWS 11:1

Each day, we exercise our faith in others. We place our lives in the hands of doctors, trust our children's safety to educators, and believe the motorist in the other lane will obey the traffic laws.

For the Christian, faith is as essential as breathing. In Romans 1:17, Paul says the righteous shall live by faith. Our faith is Christ-centered. Enveloped by His love, we trust Him to instruct, protect, and guide us daily.

We demonstrate our faith in Him when we are willing to give Him the keys to our lives and allow Him to steer the course.

CAUTION FLAG

When we approach God, we first must believe that He exists as the eternal Father and that He will answer our prayers. Without faith, we cannot fully please Him (Heb. 11:6).

CIRCUIT RIDER

Darlington Raceway is recognized as one of the toughest race courses in the world, requiring drivers to negotiate four very different turns on an oblong track that is narrow and unforgiving.

PIT STOP

Only God can give us faith. It is never earned. The Bible tells us that Jesus is the "author and finisher of our faith" (Heb. 12:2).

CHAPTER TWELVE

Endurance

THE PEOPLE WORKED WITH ALL THEIR HEART.
(NEHEMIAH 4:6, NIV)

May 30, 1999, was one of the biggest days of Tony Stewart's career.

A NASCAR rookie, Stewart participated in one of auto racing's most dramatic double-headers on the Sunday of Memorial Day weekend. He drove in the Indianapolis 500 in Indiana and then flew to Charlotte, North Carolina, to race in the Coca-Cola 600 on the same day.

It was a remarkable and unprecedented achievement. Stewart fell a few miles short of completing eleven hundred grueling racing miles in one day, finishing ninth at Indianapolis and fourth at Charlotte.

At the end of a tiring Sunday, Stewart was celebrated as a singular racer, one able to endure the mental and physical hardships associated with driving in two of the world's toughest motor sports events on the same day.

Two separate teams of mechanics had prepared and maintained the two cars that Stewart raced on the big day. His Indy-car team worked on his 500 car for weeks and kept it in tune while Stewart was away racing on the Winston Cup tour, his primary focus.

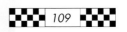

Stewart's NASCAR team, owned by Joe Gibbs, kept his stock cars in top condition while Stewart bounced back and forth from Charlotte to Indianapolis to other Winston Cup racing locations, juggling Winston Cup qualifying and racing and Indianapolis testing and qualifying.

A full roster of team personnel, sponsor representatives, and public relations people were involved in the intense planning and logistics that enabled Stewart to race in Indianapolis and then board a private jet to fly to Charlotte. They also coordinated a ride on a helicopter from the airport to the speedway and helped him arrive at all locations on time.

The day, which was more successful than Stewart could have dreamed, proved that anything can be accomplished with dedication, preparation, and cooperation. Though he endured much and needed help climbing out of his stock car at day's end, the reward at the final stop was beyond measure.

Enduring Hardships

Therefore, my beloved brethren, be steadfast, immovable, always abounding in the work of the Lord, knowing that your labor is not in vain in the Lord.
1 Corinthians 15:58

Seemingly impossible tasks require endurance.

To endure the difficult hardships that accompany great tasks, you must have dedication and loyal supporters who believe in your dream.

The Book of Nehemiah records the leadership of Nehemiah, a man who sought to rebuild the walls of Jerusalem to protect it again. The task bordered on the impossible, but Nehemiah believed that God had given him this dream and that He would give him the help and support to complete the task.

Nehemiah's plan fell into place. He received a leave of absence from his work as cupbearer to the king of Persia, and the timber to rebuild the wall was provided. Then, Nehemiah and his loyal supporters endured the hardships of this tough job, working from dawn to dark. Even though some people violently opposed their work, the men plowed on through every problem, not even stopping to change clothes.

In fifty-two days, the wall was rebuilt, and the dream became reality. When their enemies heard of it, they were disheartened because they knew the work was done by God (Neh. 1–6).

We should persevere when our tasks seem difficult and beyond our strength. When God chooses us to carry out His plans, He will also give us support and will help us endure.

CAUTION FLAG

Remember those who endure hardships with you. They are God's instruments of support.

CIRCUIT RIDER

The Coca-Cola 600 in Charlotte, North Carolina, is the Winston Cup season's longest race. It starts in the bright sun of afternoon and finishes under the lights.

PIT STOP

No task is too big for God. Approach life's big roadblocks with the certain knowledge that He is with you.

CONCLUSION

Courage. Patience. Determination. Endurance. Faith. These are the qualities of a winning racer—and attributes valuable to everyday living.

The pursuit of the ideal is a weekly quest for NASCAR racers; it should also be the goal of each person in the Christian walk. Often the road is difficult, but the pauses along the way—pit stops, if you will—can help. Stop, and let God's Word be the guide for the next step.

Race car drivers—those tough people who must deal with danger, a frantic lifestyle, and emotional ups and downs—also benefit from quiet moments in the Word.

Stevie Waltrip, wife of veteran NASCAR driver Darrell Waltrip, decided almost twenty years ago to provide an unusual weekly source of inspiration for her husband while he engaged in some of the most intense and successful racing of his long career.

Stevie had experienced a rejuvenation in her Christian life and was gaining a new love for the Scriptures. She wanted to share her joy with Darrell in a very real, personal way.

"The Bible will change your heart," she said. "It will change your attitude. You never know what's going to happen during a race. You prepare and do the best you can do. But there's a certain amount that's left up to what's going on around you. I wanted Darrell to take some of the Scriptures with him."

Stevie started picking a Scripture verse each week, writing it on an index card, and leaving it inside Darrell's car prior to the start of that week's race. It became a tradition, one the Waltrips have continued for hundreds of races for almost twenty years.

"Sometimes I try to match the Scripture with a problem he might be having," she explained. "Sometimes I just open the Bible to Psalms and pick one. It probably helps me as much as it helps Darrell."

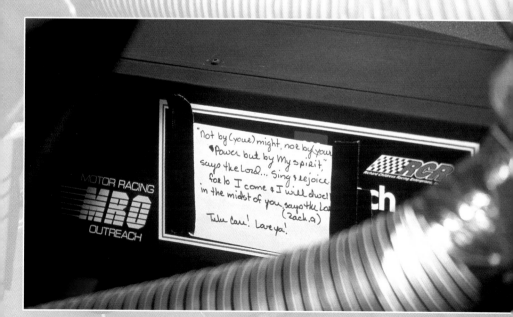

Driver Dale Earnhardt once noticed Stevie holding a Scripture card before a race. Stevie remembers, "He asked me what I was doing, and I told him I always write Scripture and put it in Darrell's car before the race. He said, 'Well, where's mine?' I said, 'Well, right here!' So I wrote him one, and I've been doing it ever since."

On the road of life, in times good and bad, we ride easier with the knowledge that God travels the same path, ever available for guidance, instruction, and comfort. In His love and in His Word, we run the most important race of all.

APPENDIX

Motor Racing Outreach

HE FLEW UPON THE WINGS OF THE WIND.

(PSALM 18:10)

The stock car racing community is a village on wheels. It stops at one speedway; stays there for three or four days during practice, qualifying, and racing; then moves on to the next city. For most of the year, drivers, crew members, and NASCAR officials and their families are on the road.

For many people in racing, Motor Racing Outreach (MRO) is the place they can call home away from home. Established in 1988, MRO is an interdenominational ministry that serves the racing community and all its members.

Since most races are held on Sundays, drivers and team members seldom have the opportunity to attend traditional church worship services. MRO brings that experience to the speedway, offering chapel services in the garage area in the hours before each race.

In addition to organizing church services, MRO provides a mobile community center for racing families. A large transporter arrives at virtually every race site during race week, and a few hours later the trailer and its

adjacent covered areas have been transformed into a gathering place and play area for children associated with race teams. The staff organizes programs and activities for the racers' children and operates a physical rehabilitation center where team members can receive help from athletic trainers.

The mobile facilities also have quiet places where drivers and others can meet with MRO staff members. Counselors are available to meet with any member of the racing community to discuss problems or assist with difficulties. Their services are particularly valuable during times of stress in what is often a dangerous sport.

On Saturday nights prior to races, MRO sponsors Bible studies for drivers. And away from the racetracks, MRO coordinates Bible studies at twenty-eight Winston Cup racing shops located in and around Charlotte, North Carolina, the hub of NASCAR racing. Program leaders visit each of the shops weekly to present studies on Bible principles or life issues during lunch breaks.

Based near Charlotte, MRO has about thirty full- and part-time staff members and numerous

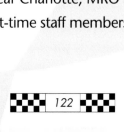

volunteers. The organization was started by and continues to be led by Max Helton, a former pastor who worked with professional athletes and recognized a need for an ongoing religious emphasis in the racing community.

Helton, the senior chaplain of MRO, says the organization stresses its services to racers and their families and emphasizes its "ministry of hanging out."

"That's what we call it," he explains. "We're there for them. We're available to talk. We hang out in and around the garage. We're available. If they need our help, we'll try to help. If they want to talk about their relationship to God, we're there."

Immediately before each race, Helton and other MRO personnel pray individually with drivers.

But MRO's impact does not stop with the racing community. The organization also operates Racing Fans Outreach (RFO), a ministry to the millions of fans who attend races across the country. RFO schedules race-day worship services outside speedways at many of the stops on the Winston Cup schedule.

Not limited to Winston Cup racing, MRO also ministers in other forms of NASCAR competition, other auto racing series, motorcycle racing, and boat racing.

Assisting Drivers

Young driver Adam Petty, following in the racing footsteps of his great-grandfather Lee Petty, his grandfather Richard Petty, and his father Kyle Petty, faced an immense challenge during the 1998 season.

Petty's crew chief was killed in a pit-road accident during a short-track race in Minnesota. The death of his close friend and teammate hit Petty hard, but his father said his Christian faith helped him through the difficult time.

"I think we've been very fortunate to have been around Motor Racing Outreach and that Patti (Adam's mother) has taken the kids to church in their younger years," Kyle said. "He has a great faith, a really strong faith in Christ. And I think we all do—that helped him as much as anything."

Cup Series
BRISTOL
NASCAR Winston
ty Care
88
THUNDERBIRD
76
WISECO